```
Little
Tales of
Strange
Behaviour
_____

John
Staunton
```

Copyright John Staunton 2021
staunton.jb@gmail.com
Cover: frog (PD) photograph

To my kids, Matilda and Woody;
I hope you get a kick out of reading
these stories, as much as I did out of
writing them__

And, to Sharon, my wife;
for her kindness and love, for
putting up with me, and allowing
me the freedom to exist
in the world of fiction__

By the same author

Fiction

The Deathbed & Other Stories
The Observational Rantings of a Realist (as Will Levi)

Poetry

Hiding in the Safety of Things
The Good and the Dead
The Crafty Art of Creation

Plays

(THREE PLAYS)
How I Married a Monkfish!
Crabtree's Last Stand
Nuthouse

(TWO PLAYS)
Comedy of Horrors
What Happened to Bunny Melmoth?

All available from
amazon.com

THE SNAILS	8
THE SINGER	13
THE GIRL IN THE GLASS COFFIN	16
THE WRITING CLASS	19
THE UNDEAD BAKER	23
THE TRANSFORMATION	26
THE BEST-SELLING AUTHOR	30
THE SEX THERAPIST	33
THE PARACHUTE JUMP	38
THE GIFT	41
THE DEATH SENTENCE	45
THE POCESSION OF PENELOPE CROFT	49
THE BARKING MAN	52
THE POND	56
THE ACTRESS	59
THE HORRIBLE, UNSPEAKABLE DAY	62

THE PLUMBER	66
THE COTTAGE INDUSTRY	70
THE RIP OFF	76
THE UGLIEST WOMAN IN TOWN	79
THE AD MAN	82

PREFACE

The artist is the creator of beautiful things.

Those who find ugly meanings in beautiful things are corrupt without being charming. This is a fault.

Those who find beautiful meanings in beautiful things are cultivated. For these there is hope.

There is no such thing as a moral or an immoral book. Books are well written, or badly written. That is all.

No great artist ever sees things as they really are. If he did he would cease to be an artist.

There are two ways of disliking art. One is to dislike it. The other is to like it rationally.

Lying, the telling of beautiful untrue things, is the proper aim of art.

When critics disagree the artist is in accord with himself.

All art is useless.

Oscar Wilde

THE SNAILS

'Do you like eating snails, Susan?'

What a horrible thing to say to me. To ask such a question. Of course I don't like eating snails. They are my pets, my babies. I sometimes wonder what I am paying him for. I don't know why he is still confused. They go everywhere with me. I keep about fifteen of them - with a head of lettuce - in my handbag.

Some people do eat snails. I know this to be a fact. I am not stupid. They are unfeeling and they have no breeding. They mostly live in France. A place I never want to visit. You've seen one Eiffel Tower you've seen them all.

His name is Dr Bernard Goodman. I've been going to him for eighteen years. He isn't a very good psychiatrist. He has loads of letters after his name; and he looks the part. Most of his patients are easily fooled and are happy to keep coming to him. The room is cosy. The couch is comfortable. And there is always a box of Kleenex on the coffee table.

He's not bad looking, I suppose. A bit frayed around the edges. Not exactly what you would call ripe for love. But when we get married I can cook and I can clean and I can keep house for him. I will be able to take care of his every need.

'You're daydreaming again, Susan. Did you remember to take all your tablets since the last time I saw you?' I bet she didn't.

My job would be so much easier if they all just took their tablets. Susan has been my patient for a long time. She is beyond help. She is - as we like to say in the profession - a real nut-job, a fruitcake.

In the right light, I suppose, she could be seen as an attractive woman; a few candles burning and after a glass or two of red wine. She is pleasing to look at, quite passable for her age. If only she hadn't got so many mental problems.

I think he's drunk. He smells of drink most of the time. I know he hides bottles of alcohol in his filing cabinet. I hope when we are married he won't prove to be nothing but a handful and a disappointment.

I hope not.

He will have to allow me to bring my snails with me. They go where I go; they are my babies.

I see him looking at me. Undressing me. I am quite an attractive woman. I know I have my problems; but who hasn't got their problems? We know everything about each other. We have no secrets. It was obvious from the beginning it was more than my mind that he was interested in. He likes to hypnotize me, to put me under. The last time when I woke up my bra was on back to front.

'We are making wonderful progress, Susan. Today is an important day for us.'

Asking Susan did she eat slugs was a clever move. The face she made when I asked her was priceless. I see it as a breakthrough. It momentarily shocked her out of her stupidity. She has to realise that a relationship with slugs is a filthy and unnatural obsession. I think I saw one of the slimy little creatures sticking its head out of her coat pocket.

My babies are sad when I am not home. They stay hidden in their shells and wait for me to return. Every day I let them out on the kitchen table for some exercise. They are constantly breeding, laying eggs. They can lay up to six batches a year, with over eighty eggs per batch. Bless their little tentacles. They get into all sorts of places: behind the cooker, in the laundry basket, even under my pillow! The little rascals.

Watching snails is so relaxing; they just slither around at their own pace enjoying their surroundings. The oldest girl I have is Doris. She is seven years old. She has got very poor eyesight, but an amazing sense of smell; she is always able to recognize me. They love to have their shells rubbed; they also like to be rubbed around the head and neck. They make such funny faces when they are eating. You can't keep just one snail. They are very social creatures. They need friends. They love to have a warm bath with me on the weekends.

I see Susan has brought her suitcase with her today. This is good. She is composed and seems relaxed. She looks elegant and stylish. But it takes more than a new hairdo and a bit of lipstick to fool a professional like me. I have seen this type of behaviour before with women and their cats. But never with slugs. In the profession we call it: Spinster Syndrome, or OMD: Old Maids Disorder.

I must be gentle. Susan is a fragile woman. Those beautiful and wild and dangerous eyes of hers are a dead giveaway. God only knows what a mad person is capable of. I once spotted a head of iceberg and a carving knife in her handbag.
I must be careful.
I must show a semblance and a suggestion of sensitivity and sincerity. If it wasn't for those damn slugs! They disgust me! The slimy mucus-headed revolting little bastards! I can't even imagine how much they all eat, and where they all poop!

Why doesn't he just pop the question? We both know why we are here on a Sunday. The flowers and the chocolates and the bottle of champagne are probably in his filing-cabinet. How romantic! I know Bernard likes snails too. And in time he will grow to love them as much as I do.

'Susan, you do know what is happening? You do know why we are here today?' Susan sat smiling, fondling the contents of her handbag.

'I am no longer able to help you. I have tried my best; but you have me stumped. The ambulance is on its way here as we speak. The hospital is the right place for you. It's time now for the experts.'

The piercing scream-like sound, like that of a mortally wounded animal, could be heard throughout the whole building.

THE SINGER

Sometime after Willy Coombs had died a shoe-box was found filled with old tape cassettes. He had hoped to blossom like an exotic flower, or some sort of rare butterfly, and to transform into a great singer. He wished to soar. He wanted nothing more than to be loved.

He sung so badly, it upset people. It actually annoyed them. As soon as he would start singing, he was told to stop. The sound was like that of a cat being strangled, or long nails being dragged across a blackboard.

'I long to sing as long as the day is long,' he used to say. 'I sing in my sleep. I dream of singing in front of an audience and winning a big competition. I sing in the shower. I sing in the bath. I sing when I'm having a pee; and when I'm having a poo.' He was not a normal person. Some people called him retarded.

Everything he learned he learned from listing to other singers. People saw him each day walking to and from work, singing loudly - in the wrong key and the wrong tempo - with his headphones and walkman at full volume. Cole Porter was his favourite.

He found it hard to make friends. 'I get so depressed when I'm not singing,' he'd tell people. 'My head feels empty and full of air. I need my music to fill up my brain and to keep the non-singing voices away.'

The tape cassettes found in the shoe-box after he died are amateur and unlistenable. He had recorded the cassettes in his bedroom over many years. Hundreds of bits and pieces of music and songs. Endless recordings of noise and sounds.

Willy had lived all his life at home with his mother. She was an overweight and unhappy woman who stayed in bed a lot. A strict and religious woman. She prayed every day for many hours in front of a large crucifix. She had never married. Willy came to her late in life. He was looked upon as a blessing; God's gift to her. The father was never mentioned or talked about.

Willy Coombs had a severe stutter and a lisp. When he talked it sounded like gibberish and nonsense. Over time he found it easier not to talk. Except for the singing, he became a selective mute. He was born with one leg shorter than the other; which when he walked gave him the appearance of being drunk. He never drank in his life. His body had no tolerance for alcohol. The day the motorcycle hit him he was listening to Frank Sinatra singing, at full blast, I Get A Kick Out Of You.

'When I sing, I am uplifted,' he recorded on a tape found in the shoe-box, 'I am transformed by the splendour of the song; I am transported to a better place. I feel the emotion that is denied to me in everyday life.' His voice on the tape was difficult to understand (because of his severe speech impediment; but, with perseverance and time, it became easier to make out).

He worked in the fish factory for 23 years. He smelled of fish. The local bus driver stopped picking him up because of the complaints. He wasn't the fastest fish gutter in the factory, but he worked hard, and he never looked for a pay rise. He'd bring fish home every day (mackerel was his favourite; he loved the taste of it; and the way the sunlight magically bounced off their scales). The house reeked of fish-heads and guts.

'Why can't you get a nice job in a sweet factory or a cake shop,' his mother would say, 'and bring me home some bon bons and some custard slices, instead of that damn fish all the time!'

It is true, Willy did lack technique, and he lacked training. He had the worst singing voice in the world. BUT HE NEVER STOPPED SINGING. He had a need to be heard; a voice deep down inside him that needed to be listened to. The cruel faith of a lisping and stuttering singer: to have all the sensitivity of a great artist, but none of the talent.

'If people could only hear what I hear when I sing,' he said on the tape recording, 'they'd hear nothing, but joy! That'll do me. I will settle for that. They can keep the talent – I will have the joy!'

THE GIRL IN THE GLASS COFFIN

They all queued in a single line to stare at the girl in the glass coffin. It was a hot, uncomfortable day. The sun cut through the stain-glass windows in the church. They all took turns to look into the coffin. It was an open invitation and opportunity. The students were confused, and curious, at the same time. Some parents were unhappy with the body displayed in a glass coffin; they thought it too traumatic, too disturbing; that it would lead to unpleasant, uninvited memories.

Her father believed it would bring home the reality of the loss; as the sudden death had left him with a sense of unreality. He also believed that when her mother died (three years ago from cancer, after a long and terrible illness) - that nothing could ever be as bad again.

Carol lay there exposed for all to see. She had been a kind and soft-hearted girl, with the saddest blue eyes; always so meek and gentle. She was dressed in the lilac and pink gown she had picked for her graduation.
The father wept.
A weeping that would not subside. It was as if a hammer had fallen from the sky and onto his head. An instant destruction: like his heart had been ripped out of his ribcage.

As the father looked into the coffin, for one long and very strange moment, he thought his daughter was alive again. She looked beautiful; her skin was pink and smooth; her hair neatly groomed. Even her fingernails were painted, and she had a small smile on her face. He knew she was dead. But at that moment, he thought she may sit up and look at him. The experience left him wondering: why do they make a dead person appear so alive? They make the body look, more or less, not dead.

The glass coffin was his choice. He wanted the world to see her beauty, one final time. To see her at her best. Before the ground, and before time, would destroy it all. Before his memories would fade, and she would no longer exist.
He noticed her skin was very cold and hard when he kissed her goodbye.

The home turned into the saddest of houses. No invites were given out; nobody visited. Carol's room was untouched and never entered into. A beautiful daughter gone. To be no more. And a parent with no belief in God - or of any better place - called heaven.
It was a pain with no remedy, and no relief.

For almost six months before her death, Carol was preparing to die. She did this systematically, by organizing everything in her room; and slowly saying goodbye to friends and family in an unsentimental and knowing way. Mostly she tried to make sense of it all. The unremarkable life she had lived.

Her entire existence seemed for nothing. She tried to keep her spirit alive by reading her favourite books (she loved the novels of Jane Austen in particular); but her mind wondered in too many directions; and this saddened her - as reading had been such solace to her in the past. To talk about her private feelings was difficult for her. She was a young girl without hope, filled with loneliness and despair. She was drowning, daily; anchored by a terrible and unfathomable sadness.

A dark place she could not escape from.

Four years later the father decided to decorate Carol's bedroom. He picked a warm shade of pink for the walls. On her bedside locker, he placed a glass vase, filled with fresh lilacs and roses. For a brief moment, he felt at ease; even a little proud.

On a shelf behind a collection of books, he found a little cloth bag, tied with a purple ribbon; inside was a small fabric doll - it was the worry doll he had given to her - just after her mother had died. Also in the bag was a folded piece of paper.

The father sat on the end of her bed; and cried, when he read the note:

I just want the pain to stop. To be able to look in the mirror without crying. I am ugly. UGLY! UGLY! UGLY!

THE WRITING CLASS

Sarah paused to inspect herself in the bathroom mirror. A girl with a nice body and a pretty face stood reflected there, with medium-sized breasts that stood up proudly in her halter top. She gave her long straight cinnamon hair a perky toss and decided Joe would be crazy to even think of ever letting her go.

This is the type of shit I have to put up with every week. It's not like I cannot turn up; I am the facilitator of the group. I've hardly a brain cell left at this stage. It's impossible for me to remain encouraging; or to look half-interested anymore. The fact is: the majority of the fools can't write. They should not be let anywhere near a pen and paper, never mind a computer.

She remembered to spray under her arms, and on her secret place, with her favourite deodorant, before entering the room where Joe lay naked on the bed. She walked to the bed and looked at the different parts of his body, starting from the bottom: feet, ankles, knees, crotch, and midriff. Joe's tumid penis sprang to freedom like a Jack-in-the-Box.

It's like an AA meeting. All sitting around looking for attention and adulation. If it's not drink, then it's some kind of a mental problem. They are all needy. Different layers and levels of madness; a collaboration of losers.

Why do they all want to bloody write?

More importantly: Why do they all think that they *can* write? Not one of them has a built-in shit-detector. Their last drafts look like a first draft.

Everything they write is a sure-fire cure for insomnia. They wouldn't know craft if it crawled up their leg and bit them on the arse.

I destroyed most of my stories and poems, and a very bad novel, years ago. More people should do this.

The twitter of the blue-birds was heard just outside the window, which looked out on a soft green landscape bathed in the warming light of the setting amber sun. She smiled at him as he lay beside her, and she could see all their many tomorrows bringing her happiness such as she felt right now.

We meet every Thursday in a small room at the back of the church. On average ten people take the course. I charge a twelve-week fee (for the rent of the room; and enough left for me to get drunk on the way home). I used to teach a class in Nineteen-Century English & Russian Literature in a well-known and influential college.

My students were some of the best young writers. (I'd hand-pick six new students a year from an applicant pool of between four and five hundred.) They'd arrive already wonderful; I merely, over the three years, helped them to develop their 'writing voice'.

It ended badly.

All I will say is: students are not to be believed. I was involved in no wrongdoings. I was a scapegoat. Some young students have over fertile minds, and grudges to bear. For example, if I gave them a low grade, they would often try to encourage me to give them a better grade. Some of the young female students were very persuasive.

"What's wrong?" He asked, as he sat up straight in the crumpled bed. "You have a wounded look in your eyes that makes me think you're going through some painful issues."

"Yes, my husband has been cold to me for years, so I've decided to make a break with him and start fresh," she told him, as she fondled his chest. "And now that you have shown me what a real man is like, I think I'm falling hopelessly, and helplessly, in love with you!"

This lot are dumb. They have no voice. They are much older. They see the class as a substitute for a weekly gardening or knitting group. They have no passion for literature, they are not dedicated readers, and they've no understanding of the way the creative process works.

They know nothing about character, exposition, motivation, action, or resolution. The great writers like: Joyce, Chekov, Tolstoy, Hemingway, and Kafka, are foreign to them. I give them homework. God help me! I wish the proverbial canine would chew it up before I have to look at it! It's pitiful and painful to read. Actually, I just take a glance at it, stick a high mark on it, and pretend I've read it.

After the twelve weeks, I give them all a certificate. It means nothing and it is useless. But it makes them feel good about themselves.

Sarah and Joe embraced, making love to each other one more time. "He's such a stud," she thought, as she orgasmed for the fifth time that morning. She gently played with Joe's joystick, realising how lucky she was. "He makes me feel so good," she thought to herself, "I've been feeling bloated and constipated for the last few days, but all that rigorous lovemaking has sorted all that out."

They were now both exhausted. The salty sweat glistened and rolled off their hot naked bodies. They now both had such plans to set into immediate motion, such perfect, wonderful plans. The future was theirs and theirs alone. It was beyond doubt that they would not remain together.

Their love was true, and strong, and as timeless, as the rugged cliffs on the shoreline, outside their bedroom window.

THE UNDEAD BAKER

My name is Barney Poole. I am 62 years old.

And I died a few hours ago.

As I rest here on this table, before they do whatever it is they have to do to me, I'd like to tell you a little bit about myself, and how I got into this pickle in the first place.

I was in my garden, pruning my roses, when this dreadful pain travelled down my right arm. It was awful; I wouldn't wish it on my worst enemy (not that I have any enemies; I like people, and they seem to like me, I think). Anyway, that's when I fell to the ground, nearly impaling myself on my secateurs.

Now I am dead.

I know this to be a fact. Yet I remain conscious; my brain is still very much alert. But it is no longer able to control my body. I tried wiggling my big toe a minute ago, the one they put the tag on, but it won't move a jot. I also feel cold; and a bit achy and stiff.

I'm a positive person. Things have changed, and there's nothing I can do about it. I see - without being able to move my head, or my eyes - that there are 3 other corpses in here with me. I don't know if their brains are still alive. I may be the only one who's aware of what's going on.

I overheard 2 of the staff talking about me.

"We should make a start on this one," one of them said, "he's beginning to leek a bit and stink up the place."

"No rush, no fuse; he's going nowhere," the other one said, in-between mouthfuls, "as soon as I finish my chicken and stuffing sandwich." The cheeky monkeys!

They mean no harm; they are young.

It looks like I took a heart attack. That's what I think must have happened. I'm not a medic, but that would be an educated guess, judging by the pain in my arm. I can't remember taking a ride in an ambulance. I can't remember any doctors or nurses trying to resuscitate me or give me the kiss of life. I'm not complaining. There is always somebody worse off than you are.

I had a little bakery shop just off the main street. I got up every morning with the lark; you could hear me whistling a tune, or singing a song, on my way to work as the sun came up. O, deary me! I just thought of all my customers turning up for their fresh crusty turnovers. That's not like me at all. My shop is never closed! And I didn't cancel the milkman or the newspapers! There'll be a big pileup in my front porch! It's all going to look very inconsiderate.

I am trying to remain optimistic. I'm in no pain. But I am a cold (there's no heating on in here, and the sheet over me is very flimsy). I'm also hungry; there's a strange rumbling noise coming from my tummy. The room is sparse and dreary (to be fair, it does look clean, and all the tables are stainless steel). The place could do with a bit of cheering up. A lick of paint. Maybe a small TV up on the wall, to relieve some of the boredom.

"1 2 3 ... Up we go!" said one of the workers as he lifted me off the table and put me into the coffin. "They never get any lighter," the other one said as he put the lid on, "no matter what size they are, they all weigh a bloody ton!"
Then they nailed the lid shut.

It's my own fault I'm in this predicament. I have been foolish. I should've done more exercise, and eaten a few less chocolate éclairs. I wouldn't call myself fat. I have a bit of a saggy belly. And big ankles; I've always had big ankles.

I wished I had learned how to paint, or that I had taken-up flower arranging. Oh, well - there's no point on dwelling on what cannot be undone. I had a good life. I was the way I was, for better or worse; and now I'm leaving happily, to re-join something bigger.

It's quiet now. Darker.
I faintly can hear voices, mumblings. I hear footsteps. I think I am being carried somewhere.

It looks like I won't be needing an autopsy, or have to be embalmed. I'm glad of that. I imagine it would be quite invasive, and a bit embarrassing.

I guess, since I have no family or next of kin there's no need to hold things up. Now I am hot. I can smell cooking, like a Sunday roast. I hear a crackling sound.

Whether I'll be better or worse off when I get to where I am going, or whether I'll be disappointed or find there what I expect, you will all learn soon enough.

THE TRANSFORMATION

Franz Gogol woke up one morning and discovered he had turned into a giant donut. There was nothing but a large hole where his insides used to be. He rubbed his eyes to see if he was awake. At first, he was dumbfounded; then flabbergasted. After he got used to the idea, he rolled himself out of bed, and onto the floor. 'Perhaps,' he thought, 'the big lump of cheese I ate late last night is the reason for this occurrence? After thinking about it for some time, he thought about it no more.

He had apple juice for breakfast. It made him feel soggy and damp. It was not a nice feeling. 'I should not eat or drink anything at present,' he thought, 'not until I get a better handle on things.' He did not want people to see him; so he stayed home and watched television; and slept.

A few days later, after finishing a cup of coffee (which was a strange sensation), he decided to go into town. It had stopped raining. He was thankful for that. He rolled along, picking up pace, as he went. Nobody noticed, or bothered him. He caught his reflection in a shop window. It was not the correct shape for a man at all.

'I need to find a new job,' he thought, 'or register myself as disabled?' Lately, even before Franz Gogol had changed into a donut, he had lost a lot of confidence in himself. He was bored and cleaning windows for a living.

'But what work can a donut do?' He asked himself. 'No! This is not the right way to look at things. I can do anything I put my mind to. Change is not always a bad thing.'

He entered the employment office, trying to look as normal as he could, under the circumstances. The amount of stairs frightened him so he waited and took the elevator. He went into the room and gave his name and other relevant details to a clerk behind a screen. The clerk, no more than 18 years old, had a shiny red and over-washed face. He believed his rank to be higher than it was. He liked to ask awkward questions.
'Do you drive?'
'Are you willing to travel?'
'There are more vacancies and opportunities if you drive and if you are willing to travel,' He said.
Franz answered yes to everything he was asked. He did not want to come across as lazy, or seem uninterested.
"Do not look so worried and nervous, just relax,' the clerk said, with a smile that looked more like a grimace.
'We do not judge here. All of our positions are of equal opportunities, and are open to all.' He looked at Franz Gogol and saw the bored and glazed look his eyes.
'That's great, that's very good,' Franz said.
But he didn't think it was great or very good at all. The clerk had put him on edge and made him feel worthless. Franz did not drive. He had never driven a day in his life. And it was too late to learn now.
'I need hands, and I need legs, to be able to drive,' he thought. Then he panicked, and fled from the office; bouncing down the stairs and out onto the street nearly knocking down a women and her dog.

He made it home. He was tired; he lay on the couch. He was upset. On his way home a small child had tried to take a bite out of him. It had upset him that the mother did not reprimand the child; she merely laughed and went on her way.

He knew he would never be able to work again.

Franz could feel himself getting smaller. He was shrinking little by little; leaving crumbs everywhere he went. He did not know how to eat. And he had very little appetite.

'Why couldn't I have turned into something else instead of a donut?' he thought. 'A donut, for god's sake! It's ridiculous! I never even had a sweet tooth! Now I have no teeth!

The whole thing is inconceivable!'

He was embarrassed. He covered the long mirror in his bathroom with a towel. He missed wearing his clothes most of all. He used to have style; the right clothes, the right shoes, made him feel good, important.

'This is no good,' he thought. 'I look absurd! Who would want to date a donut?' He hated everything about himself: the shape; the doughy texture; the big empty hole – he hated all of it!

'I wish I had turned into a block of cheese! That would have been more dignified; I would've been more whole; I would have matured better. I could see myself sitting with a glass of red wine in front of the fire. Why did I have to turn into this soulless and greasy waste of a life!

He worried people would no longer take him seriously. No longer respect him. That they'd make fun of him; make him the butt of every joke. The truth is: nobody ever did take Franz Gogol seriously. Nobody actually thought about him at all. He was not an important man.

Most people were not even aware of his existence.

THE BEST-SELLING AUTHOR

Every barfly and street-corner gossip will tell you they can write a book. They have so much to say, so much experience, been so many places, seen so many things. But they don't write. They can't. All they can do is talk. They sit and drink and stand around and waste time and talk. The non-writing writers. The pontificators of drivel and hogwash. The procrastinators of piss-poor ideas.

Save me from these.

You must be ready to piss blood in order to be a bestselling author. My first novel, *The Dead Don't Laugh*, was a huge success. I was twenty-four when it was published. I am now eighty. I have written seventeen books since then.

I was lucky to have had a bad childhood. This made me a good writer. Dedication and diligence and drudgery. That's what is needed. The drug of writing is a dangerous and wonderful thing. I write big books. I spend over three years on each book. I am a hardback tougher bred; not a mere paperback hack.

Writing is not a natural thing. It is as hard as learning to play the piano. I would never encourage anybody to write. For the same reason I could not listen to the wrong notes being played on a piano.

These days bad writing is enjoyed like fast food; readers know nothing else; they do not want to think; they do not like the weighty literature of the serious novel. And so the sludge piles up on the overfilled bookshelves.

I am blessed in knowing how good a writer I am. I write for the writing. And damn the readers. I need no readers. They get in the way. The work is everything. I write to clear the thoughts in my head; I put them on the page and am done with them. It purges me. I am my own reader. I am the hardest critic, the best judge of my work. If it satisfies me, I have done my job well. My goal is precision, and the pursuit for perfection.

Publishing houses are brothels, editors are whoremasters, and critics are the prostitutes riddled with the clap. I learned to write, by writing. I force myself every day, and I forge on. It has left me with a bad nervous system, but not a shortened life. I haven't submitted a manuscript in over forty years. I won't be told what to write, like a trained seal, waiting for fish-heads to be flung at me. I pander to no fad or market. I am not in it for the money or the glory.

I have remained productive through the decades. The work is a blessing. I am my own muse. I need no other. I have stamina. You don't write novels by putting in two hours a week or by having too many hangovers. I am no amateur.

I write with such gloom and such dissatisfaction; I finish each book mentally and physically drained. A black mood hangs over me for months. Until I start the next book. And so it continues; and the madness prevails.

I am lucky: I do not like people; I am unsociable. I prefer every day to face a blank piece of paper. Real people bore me. I live with the characters I create. They keep me on my toes. I have no telephone or television. I have no distraction from sitting at my desk. I still write in longhand (up to six hours each day). The next morning, I type it all up, editing as I go. I must believe the work is important. Or else why suffer the slow self-destruction that it entails.

My books are to be burnt with me. I want nothing to be left behind. I want no readers. I wrote the books for me to read. Not for other people. My first bestseller was a mistake. I do not think it was well written. I have improved.

Lately my mind is sluggish and constipated. One of the many drawbacks of old age. I may stop writing tomorrow. Tomorrow I may become a non-writer. This will be OK. I will be free. I will have nothing more to say. It will be a rest from the clutter and the continuous avalanche of words. Writing has nearly destroyed me. To be able to turn it off, shut it all down, would be wonderful. Writing so many books has made me schizophrenic. I live in a controlled state of madness; only the perception of normality, of reality, prevails. I am a depleted and worn-down human being.

A see a white room. A madman. A sage. A scribbler. The Almighty Novelist. The God of Fiction. The Creator of Letters, Words, Sentences, Paragraphs, Pages, Chapters... BOOKS! I must stop. I must stop. I must stop___
I will never stop. God help me! And keep me medicated.

THE SEX THERAPIST

'He calls it, the vagina flytrap,' the wife said, as she sat opposite the husband, 'I don't like it, it's very sexist! How'd he like it if I said he had a purple turnip headed penis!

Not one bit, I bet!'

My name is Dr. Sara Clerkin. I am a sex therapist. I talk about sex a lot. You could say I'm a very oral person. And I listen. I have to be a good listener. Some of the things they tell me would make your hair stand up on the back of your necks. Come to think of it - a lot of the men I see do have really hairy necks. The little monkeys! Forever trying to show off their little pink bottoms.

'He's constantly horny and demands sex from me! Enough is never enough,' the wife continued. 'I mean, no woman wants to be treated like a prostitute, do they? I mean, men aren't bloody fussy, are they? They'll put it anywhere; any hole, anytime__'

I listen to stuff like this all the time.

'She's always got a headache,' the husband says. 'She's never in the goddamn mood! It's always some excuse. She's inhibited, she's got no imagination whatsoever!'

It's harder when I have to put up with the couples. They are very often close to killing each other by the time they come and see me.

I shouldn't complain. I am not cheap.

I don't deal with the offenders. The molesters. Or any of the hard-core deviants. (And I don't treat politicians or priests anymore, I found them to be incurable, beyond my help.) Don't get me wrong, I still get my fair share of the weirdos. The complete A to Z of sexual pleasures, preferences and perversions. You name it. I've seen it. I used to be a shy person. Not anymore.

I have one strict rule: I never get involved with a client.

I did drop my guard once. He was so funny, he made me laugh so much, the fifty minutes would just fly by. His name was Richard - but I will call him Dick - in order to keep his anonymity and protect doctor-patient confidentiality. We spent many hours in this room together. I got to know all his fetishes and sordid little secrets. I could write a bestseller with all I have learnt over the years. Maybe someday I will. Mills & Boon with all the filthy bits left in.

He was so attractive with his designer stubble and his come-to-bed eyes and his big juicy lips. We went out together once after a very productive session. We drank a lot of wine and had a big meal. Then I took him home. Not very ethical, I know, but the mixture of the wine and the curry had lowered my defences. (I was a little embarrassed as my flat was in such a mess: dog hairs all over the place and a sink full of dirty dishes.)

It was all over before it begun.

A textbook case of penile dysfunction and premature ejaculation. He didn't even manage to get his trousers all the way down.

'I'm sorry,' he said, as he stood there whining with his limp noodle dribbling all over my carpet. 'I don't know what came over me, that never happened to me before, it must've been the wine and the black bean sauce! We can try again in a while, if you're still up for it?'

I was furious. And frustrated. A cocktail sausage would've had more meat on it. It was insulting. I called him a taxi and got rid of him. The whole episode left me with nothing but a beard rash and a dodgy stomach.

He still comes to see me. But only on a professional basis. I've discovered he is all talk. He lives purely in his own sexual fantasy world. He wouldn't know what to do with a vagina if it was handed to him on a plate.

A topic that comes up a lot is masturbation. It can cause a lot of guilt and shame. Take it from an expert: There is nothing wrong with masturbation. (Of course, it does take practice to get it right, and to get the most out of it.) People don't masturbate enough. It is a much underrated sex act. More than half of the problems I see in here could be solved if people only played with themselves more. It is free, and you don't have to get dressed up, or even leave the house to do it.

People should set aside time every day (organise yourself, and take it nice and slow) if you want to get the most out of your orgasms. I like to give people exercises and tasks. Practice does indeed make perfect.

There is also the myth: that sex without love - is an empty experience. In my experience: it is love, without sex - that leads to divorce. Romantic ideals have the world the way it is. If a man gives you a single red rose - do not be overwhelmed - it could simply mean that he is too mean to buy you the dozen.

I have one woman who comes to me that likes to be wrapped in baking parchment and fed chocolate sauce through a sieve. And a man who likes to stand naked in a bucket of custard and juggle fish fingers, while his wife is out at bingo. I kid you not. My days are never boring. One person's perversion is another person's pleasure.

Do men think about sex more often than women? Most people (mostly women) believe that they do. There is no evidence of this. The desire for sex is not gender based. There are plenty of women out there who can't walk past a fruit & veg section in a supermarket without entertaining dirty thoughts when they see a banana or a cucumber. I'm a stickler for hygiene: always wash your vegetables and fruit – before, and after use.

I did date another client. His name was John. He was a much older man. Sensitive and gentle. He was married, but unhappy. He said his wife didn't understand him. We went out together for six months. He liked to dress up in my clothes and high heel boots. But there's only so much a woman can take. And when my expensive makeup started to disappear, and he started using my tampons - I knew it was time to give him the push. He has since left his wife. He now calls himself Josephine.

Yesterday I had a breakthrough with one of my clients. He is a young gay man. He has always been scared of (and also excited by) the male organ. He was afraid to perform oral sex on his partner. 'You haven't seen the size of it,' he said. 'It's a choking hazard.' Finally, the night before last, he did it for the first time (after many hours of practice with an aubergine). He said it went swimmingly well. His partner was trilled, over the moon.

I was delighted he was able to pull it off.

I told him he must now keep it up, as one swallow, does not make a summer.

I am in a long-term relationship at the moment. We met at a church fate and hit it off immediately. We love and respect each other. The sex is out of this world; we're like rabbits together. We've explored every nook and cranny of each other. There are no boundaries. We love shopping together for the latest kinky gadgets and apparatuses. Sometimes I am the man. Sometimes she is the man. We take turns.

We don't put labels on one and other.

If I've learned anything in this game: it is that rules are meant to be broken; and not to mix business with pleasure, or to take your work home with you.

THE PARACHUTE JUMP

Julie found it almost impossible to get her legs out of the plane, without the wind blowing them back in. The noise from the engine was deafening. 'SHITE!' she roared; as she fell through the sky, and then landed on the ground like a sack of potatoes.

She did a parachute jump for charity, for the blind; and she ended up in a wheelchair.

She didn't remember any of her drill. *1 thousand. 2 thousand. 3 thousand. Check canopy: Apex. Modification. Round!* She forgot it all. Falling at 120 miles an hour - and seeing the ground below accelerating up towards her - made sure of that. When she landed she was supposed to run around the chute and gather it up quickly. She forgot. The wind dragged her for another 2 miles, and into a quarry.

When Julie was in the air she was supposed to turn her body into the wind and manoeuvre her toggles left to right. She didn't. She just floated, with her legs dangling. And before making contact with the ground she was supposed to bend her knees, land, and immediately roll over. She didn't do that either.

She blacked out as soon as she jumped out of the plane. And didn't regain consciousness until 2 years later.

She remained in a hospital bed in a coma.

The first thing Julie remembers when she woke up was being fed a strawberry milkshake by a nurse and being told she would never walk again. It was a strawberry milkshake. 'I'm allergic to fuckin' strawberries,' she said; 'if things aren't bad enough, now I'll be covered in bloody blotches and hives!'

To be in a coma for 2 years is a long time. Julie had lost a lot of weight. She was always a big woman. Her husband thinks that the parachute was not big enough for her and that's why she hit the ground like a sack of potatoes. Diets never worked for Julie in the past. 'I look good now,' she said, 'I got rid of a lot of that flab and lost my jelly belly and big bum!'

Surgery was not needed. There was no point. 'Her spine is in tatters,' remarked one of the doctors. For the 2 years she just slept like a baby. She got all her nourishment from a drip. She never had to leave the bed. But she did have to wear a nappy.

Julie had let herself go. Her hair was a mess; her roots were now grey to the tips of her split ends. She looked gaunt. Losing weight does not suit everybody. 'I'll a need a hacksaw and a hedge trimmer,' she said, 'to sort these nails out and get my bikini-line back into shape!'

While she was in a coma changes were bound to happen. For one thing, her husband, Alan, moved on. He now lives with one of his students.

He teaches mathematics and biology in a college. She is 18. He is 56. But it works. They have a lot in common. They are both fascinated by the reproductive system. In fact, she is heavily pregnant. Twins, she was told. Alan is not looking forward to it. When he was married to Julie they never wanted to have kids.

Julie loved her new look and her slender figure. 'It's just a pity I can't walk around, be able to see myself in the mirror better,' she thought. Lying prostrate all day long is not good for anybody. There is only so long a person can count the cracks in a ceiling. She thought a lot about the parachute instructor. He was so confident, so cool - so sexy in his tight jumpsuit and helmet! 'Ooh, how I'd love to climb on his back and jump out of an aeroplane with him!'
She was still a woman. She still had desires.

Time moved on. And Julie left the hospital.
She has an electric wheelchair now. An excellent one. The hospital staff bought it for her after they held a special benefit night for her.
Julie regrets doing the parachute jump.
'The blind fuckers!' she says. 'If they could only all see me now! Charity can go and kiss my fucking arse!'

We all know, in time, Julie will be fine, as anger will eventually turn into acceptance.

THE GIFT

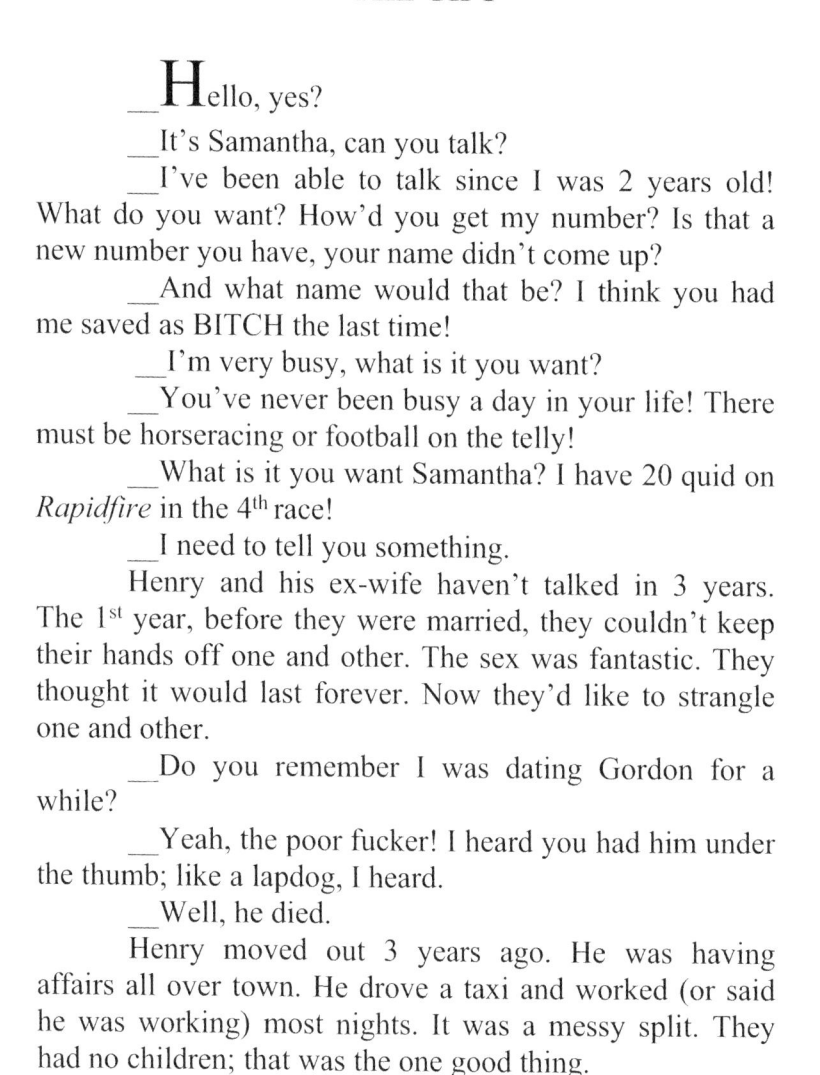

    __Hello, yes?
    __It's Samantha, can you talk?
    __I've been able to talk since I was 2 years old! What do you want? How'd you get my number? Is that a new number you have, your name didn't come up?
    __And what name would that be? I think you had me saved as BITCH the last time!
    __I'm very busy, what is it you want?
    __You've never been busy a day in your life! There must be horseracing or football on the telly!
    __What is it you want Samantha? I have 20 quid on *Rapidfire* in the 4th race!
    __I need to tell you something.

Henry and his ex-wife haven't talked in 3 years. The 1st year, before they were married, they couldn't keep their hands off one and other. The sex was fantastic. They thought it would last forever. Now they'd like to strangle one and other.

    __Do you remember I was dating Gordon for a while?
    __Yeah, the poor fucker! I heard you had him under the thumb; like a lapdog, I heard.
    __Well, he died.

Henry moved out 3 years ago. He was having affairs all over town. He drove a taxi and worked (or said he was working) most nights. It was a messy split. They had no children; that was the one good thing.

A year ago Samantha met Gordon. They fell in love almost immediately. Gordon was married before, but his wife had died a few years ago from a long illness. He was a carpenter, a hard worker. After he moved in with Samantha he fixed up the house, made it a better place. He liked to surprise her with little gifts. He made her happy. And she had loved him very much.

_You didn't poison the fucker, did you? The fool didn't eat your cooking, did he?

_That's tactless, even for you! My heart is broken here. I can't seem to find the strength to go on living. You haven't changed one bit. You're still an uncaring, no-good son-of-a-bitch!

_Ok, I give up, if he didn't die from your food, how did he die? I bet he committed suicide! That's what I'd do if I still had to live with you.

_You don't need to know all the details; his heart stopped, and he died; that's all you need to know.

Gordon actually took a heart attack, in the middle of the afternoon, while they were making love. It was the hottest day of the year. They never had sex in the afternoon before but it was his birthday. Samantha had put chocolates on his pillow and burnt perfumed oil all around the room. She also had on a garter belt and stockings and sexy panties. It was all too much for him.

He climaxed and died at the same time.

She found it difficult to get him off of her; he was a big man. He had loved his food. She used to call him her big grizzly bear.

She finally managed to free herself, and call the ambulance.

__So when's the funeral? I won't be able to go. I hate those sort of things. They depress me. It always rains in graveyards.

__He was cremated. It's done and dusted. He is sitting on my mantelpiece as we speak. It was a perfect day. The weather was lovely. I got to meet all his family. You weren't invited. You'd only have lowered the tone, and made a show of yourself, like you always do.

Henry drinks too much. He would have made a fool of himself at the funeral; especially since it was a free bar. He tries to drink only beer; as spirits turn him into a madman. He once stabbed a woman in his local pub for accidently knocking over his whiskey and & coke.

The woman is now left with a hole in her lung and wheezes when she speaks.

__You put him on the mantelpiece? You could've left the poor bastard in the ground, let him rest in peace. What is it you want, Samantha? I'm up to my eyes here.

She heard him go to the fridge and open a can of beer.

__I just wanted you to know Gordon died. That is all. But you're such a prick - I'm sorry now I even told you! He was everything to me; everything that you are not.

__Yeah, fat, and bald as a coot!

__He was a good man. He loved me. I don't know why I rang you; I guess I just wanted you to know that. Now we never have to speak to one and other again.

__Good; and make sure you delete my number from your phone.

Samantha hung up. She went over to the fireplace, and polished the urn. She was proud of how nice it looked; and amazed at how little it weighed. She laughed when she thought of how such a big man could fit so neatly inside. It made her happy to have it as a centrepiece.

Henry went back to the horseracing and had another beer and blocked her number.

6 weeks later Samantha found out she was pregnant. She was overjoyed. It was the baby she had always wanted, that she'd secretly always wished for. She thought it was impossible to conceive - because of her age and because of Gordon's obesity. Now she was going to be a mother! A real live breastfeeding mother with a pram and diapers and everything! It scared her - but she was ready.

It was the final gift from the man she loved.

THE DEATH SENTENCE

You've heard the saying: live every day as if it's your last. That's what I do. I live every day as if it's my last. I've no choice really. It's been like that for nearly 20 years. They do it on purpose. They like to make you suffer. I wish I knew the date. It would help me focus. Not knowing puts me on edge; makes me jittery. I should have taken up a hobby. If I'd known I'd still be around, I would've done.

It'll be by electric shock, or by lethal injection. I'm not too sure. They keep me guessing.

I want to get one thing straight right away. I AM NOT INNOCENT. Not by any definition of the word. So any sympathy you may have for me is wasted. Forget it. I don't need it. I don't want it. I get enough letters from women everyday wanting to marry me. I flush them all down the toilet. What sort of a messed-up mind wants to get involved with a convicted killer! There's no hope for women like that. Or men. I get letters from men as well.

The food in here is slowly killing me. It's garbage. You know the slop they give to pigs? That'd be an improvement. I'd eat that no problem. Instead of the vomit on a plate they give you here. When I don't eat it, they give out to me. I can't eat it. It makes me gag. Last week I stabbed myself with a pencil so I could go to the infirmary. The food in here is semi-normal. I may have to keep stabbing myself to stay.

They have put me on suicide watch. They took away my belt and my shoelaces and my cutlery. I'm watched like a hawk. I had a conversation with one of the wardens yesterday; he told me that they give you diapers before an execution to spare you the indignity of fouling yourself in the final moments. He also said you never forget the smell of burning when a prisoner is struck with 2,000 volts of electricity. He was full of chat and information like that.

I miss dancing most of all. I'm a marvellous dancer. You name it: tango, foxtrot or waltz, I can do it all. I have a natural rhythm. There's not enough room to dance in my cell. It's only 8x6. It's a joke. You need space to dance.

I need to find a new hobby. The other prisoners make things (mostly weapons and alcohol). Some like to make aeroplanes out of matchsticks. Not real ones, miniature ones. I don't see the point myself. It occupies their minds, I suppose.

I'm reading a book on law. (They only let you have paperbacks in here; hardbacks are considered weapons). It's called: APPEALS, LOOPHOLES & HOW TO BEAT THE SYSTEM. Every time I get to a good part they turn the lights off on me. It's all about power. They like to have control over you. I asked for a yellow highlighter and a legal a pad; they laughed at me and said 'This isn't a fuckin' Office & Supply store, Dickhead!'

The days do drag. I'll say that. We're kept in our cells 23 out of the 24 hours; with 1 hour in the yard. I asked them to leave me in my cell fulltime, but they won't. I have to mix with the lowlifes in the yard. They all want to be your friend, or to stab you in the back.

When I get back to my cell it always stinks of bleach, enough to choke a person. Most of the cells smell really bad. (Because of the body odour and the loose bowels caused by the rotten food.) But not mine. I buy the good toilet paper; I won't use the sandpaper they give you in here for free! And I keep a slow-release air freshener under my bunk.

What did I do to end up on death row, I hear you ask?

I was a kitchen porter in a hotel. I put in long hours, and was fed up of it. One night, before I left, I turned on the gas in all the cookers! The slob of a head chef was in first the following morning; I wanted to kill him with the carbon monoxide poisoning. How did I know he'd come in with a lit cigarette in his mouth! BANG! 136 residents, a night porter, and 2 chambermaids: DEAD! (Later it was discovered that night porter was in bed with both chambermaids when the explosion happened. He was always lucky like that; he never had any problem getting the girls.) There was nothing left but smoke and ash and bricks and rubble. The head chef was the first to go; I was glad to hear that.

I hope it is by lethal injection. It's more humane. They put you to sleep like a dog. The warden told me that they use a cocktail of 3 different drugs: bromide to cause muscle paralysis, chloride to stop the heart, and benzodiazepine for sedation. I have to hand it to them, they know what they're doing! It's better than getting your head shaved. A bald head does not suit everybody.

When the death sentence was handed down the jury all clapped and cheered. I distinctly heard one of them shout: 'Bring back hanging, it's good enough for the little bastard!' It'd be ironic if they decided to gas me.

But I don't think that is one of the options.

Let me just say, living on death row is no picnic; I wouldn't recommend it to anyone. And I told them they can stick their last meal - knowing my luck it'll be a bucket of vomit and a pile of pig slop!

THE POSESSION OF PENELOPE CROFT

I never wanted to be pregnant. I don't know how it happened. My husband must have got to me when I was asleep. I can't stop eating. I'm eating things I don't even like. Toothpaste and cat food. Hardboiled eggs and dog biscuits. And I pee all the time. It's degusting. I'm degusting.

Having a baby shortens your life. It ruins your body. It ages a person. The beast inside me is sucking the life out of me. It kicks me when I'm sleep. Life's tough enough without having someone kick you from the inside. I want an abortion; but they say it's too late. I will have to settle for the second choice, adoption. As soon as it's ripped out of me, it's gone.

My husband wants to keep it. He even painted the spare room and assembled a cot.
'I'll look after it, I'll do everything; you won't have to lift a finger,' he says.
It's my body. My choice. He's no say in the matter. As soon as it is birthed, it's going to an orphanage. Further away from me the better. I don't want to be a mother. I never want to see or touch a dirty nappy. Nothing is going to suck my nipples raw. I have perfect breasts; I like them exactly the way they are.

Some women are good at all that mothering stuff. Not me. I haven't a maternal bone in my body. Babies are leeches; they then grow into toddles; and then into teenagers, and even bigger leeches.

As soon as it's over, I'm leaving my husband. He bores me. He's too much work, too needy; and so annoyingly correct all the time. I'd love to kick him in the stomach and knock the bladder out of him. He should've kept his slimly tadpoles to himself; his damn demon seed! Masturbation wasn't enough for him, he had to defile me in my sleep!

Nobody knows I'm pregnant. Not the important people anyway. They see I got fat, that's all. I can't wait to get back to the un-pregnant me, back into my swimwear again. I feel like a host, with a parasite inside of it. The way a person must feel with ringworm or with nits. As soon as I've had my C-section I'm going back on the treadmill.

If a man wants a baby - he should be made grow it, and give birth to it himself; a uterus and a womb should be sewn into him. Let him carry a basketball around in this heat! Let him suffer the back pain and the heartburn!

I won't look at the baby when it is born. I don't care what sex it is. They can take it away, clean it, and bottle feed it. I won't bond with it. I know how that trap works. They make you hold it and feed it and cuddle it - hoping you'll want to keep it. That won't happen. After it's surgically removed, it will be somebody else's problem.

I bet it'll look like the father: bald head, big nose, and squinty eyes. It hasn't a hope. Some people are very forgiving; they love babies, no matter what they look like. Even the ugly ones are kept.

50

Last night I dreamt that I got rid of my husband and the baby. They were having a nap in the back seat of the car when I pushed it over the cliff. I woke up delighted.

I would never do anything like that. I'm not insane. I'm not going to jail over them.

When I fix this problem, I'll take time off work, and do some travelling. So many places to see; so much I want to do. Take a walk along the Great Wall of China, wander among the temples of Petra, snorkel the Great Barrier Reef, float in the beauty of the Dead Sea, see the spectacle of the Northern Lights___

Thing's I should have done years ago.

It will be a fresh start. I'm still relatively young. Once I get my figure back, I will be desirable again. Nobody will know the mistakes I have made. Don't dare judge me. One person's happiness, is another person's misery.

Babies and husbands are for other people. Not me.

THE BARKING MAN

Max Doberman used to be a stand-up comic. He had made a good living out of touring the circuits and the nightclubs over the years. He was funny; he always got good laughs.

Not anymore.

One night, about two years ago, he began barking in the middle of his act. It was embarrassing. He could not stop barking. He foamed and frothed at the mouth. They heckled him right off the stage. A comedian that barks - is not funny; no matter how alternative they are.

It was the last show he performed.

The barking started three years ago after his wife had divorced him. He does not bark all the time, mostly when he is stressed or anxious. It can happen anytime, anywhere. He has no control over it. His GP doesn't know what to do about it, 'I've never seen anything goddamn like it in all my years of practice,' he said. He's a useless doctor; he's near retirement and he has dementia. 'My advice,' he told him, 'is to go and see a vet!'

Max was able to hide the barking when it was only a whimper and a yelp; but now it's getting ridiculous. The barking is incessant and extremely loud. He's tried everything. He bought himself an electric shock collar. When he barked it was like licking a 9-volt battery. The shock made him bark even more. It was a vicious circle. He returned it to the pet shop and got his money back.

After the divorce Max Doberman moved out. Who got to keep the house was a real bone of contention between them; he felt he'd put a lot of work into the house and wanted to stay.

The wife got to keep the house.

She wanted shut of Max once and for all. He had never made her laugh. She never found him funny. 'I don't get it, where's the punch line?' she'd say. She was bad for his ego, his confidence. 'It's nothing but cruelty and mental torture living with a man that barks all the time,' she said.

She changed the locks on the door. She made him come back a week later to fetch his stuff from the front garden. Now he rents a bedsit, the size of a dog-box, and hasn't got enough room to swing a cat in it.

Max hadn't set foot in his wife's bedroom - never mind her double bed - in well over a year before she kicked him out. He slept downstairs on the couch. He is six foot four in his socks. He now walks with a stoop, and has developed a curved spine, from sleeping on that couch.

He saw many analysts over the years. They were full of encouragement; but there was no improvement. He just lay on the couch and whined until his time was up. One therapist gave him treats, and would say, 'there's a good boy!' in a patronizing tone. Max discovered one thing: He realized his wife had been controlling him since they were first married. She had kept him on a tight leash.

53

Metaphorically she had neutered him years ago. She often had him down on all fours picking up weeds in the garden. The neighbours knew who wore the trousers. They'd remark: 'what a loyal and obedient husband you have.'

'She's a Bitch! She took everything and left me with nothing, not even my dignity!' he told a friend, as he sat the bar barking. Max looked around the pub and saw that there were two kinds of people in the world: those who stare, and those who laugh. 'She turned me into a freak! I didn't always bloody bark! It's her fault! She's the root of all my problems!' He was agitated and barking loudly.

The barking began years ago as a nervous cough. He noticed every time his wife entered a room, or came near him, he would hyperventilate and start barking. A paper bag over his head sometimes helped. He nearly died once when his wife tried to tie a plastic bag over his head.

He loves walking in the park. He loves the open space, the fresh air. He'll stop and have a yap with all the dog owners. Dogs like him. They sniff and they lick him. (Max is not too fond of the licking and the sniffing, but he doesn't like to appear rude.) He tries hard not to bark in the park. Or on the bus. It's humiliating having a fit of barking on a crowded bus. His condition is not unique. It is similar to Tourette's, but without the bad language. There is a whole pack of other people in the world that bark. Young and old. Every race and nationality. There are even support groups. Max has no interest in meeting up with other barking people.

He used to be well groomed and smart. Now he has matted hair and a long beard. The kids on the road call him *The Wolf Man*. He lost interest in his appearance after he came out of the mental ward (six months in St. Bernard's Hospital). The treatment didn't help him much. But he did take home some nice wicker baskets and clay pots.

Today he is an old man.
He has just written his first book. A collection of jokes and one-liners. (It has given him hope as an artist; believing he can still make people laugh, means a lot to him.) He made the mistake of bringing out an audio version.

Critics can be cruel and unkind.

Max Doberman, AKA: The Barking Comic, has just brought out an audio book of new 'jokes', at the feeble age of eighty-four, went one review. *It had me howling on the floor with laughter. The man, quite literally, is barking mad! I guess that it's true - you can't teach an old dog new tricks!*

THE POND

Of all the ponds in the world why did I have to be born into this one. It is small, overcrowded and it stinks. The first day I got my legs, I jumped for joy, I was so happy. I was a tadpole no more. I was a fully grown frog with legs. I could leave this place.

My happiness did not last.

I am not stupid, I'm a realist. Frogs disappear all the time here. I hate this pond. It is dangerous. Tomorrow I could end up dead, eaten by a whole plethora of things.

My mother was an attractive frog. She was better than all the other frogs and toads. They called her a snob. She had dreams. That's what killed her. She always wanted to see the snow; she heard stories of how white and beautiful it was. One year she waited for the snow, and it came.

The cold killed her.

She drifted into a frozen hibernation and she never woke up again.

I'm still young. Two years old. Frogs can live - if we are lucky, and smart - up to ten years old. I'm dappled brown, yellow and green. A handsome frog. I have no warts. My skin is prone to dryness, so I try to stay as moist as much as possible. Dry skin is very aging. I am fully grown, which means I can leave the water and breathe the air. It would be good to leave this godforsaken pond forever.

My father was unimportant. He merely mounted my mother and covered her eggs with his sperm after she released them into the water. No finesse, no love was involved. I may have to do the same someday. I have no interest in females. I find the thought of it unpleasant. I have no wish to produce and bring more frogs into this world.

How I survived as a tadpole, I'll never know. I could've been swallowed by a fish, a bird, or even a newt. (I eat up to 70 newts and other bugs every day now. Revenge is sweet!) Life is so haphazard. The metamorphosis alone is a dangerous and vulnerable time. A lot has to go right. The lungs and the legs have to develop. Our whole body shape changes. It was a scary time. I didn't know what was happening to me. But I survived.

This is a common, dirty pond. The other frogs don't think; their minds are as stagnant as this pond. There is more to life than this. I have a brain; I can think. The other frogs merely exist. They eat. They sleep. They never contemplate the future. They haven't the intelligence to worry.

I don't like my eyes. They're bulgy, and they get sore easily. But it is the way we are made, so I accept it. I'm a great leaper. I can leap better than anybody. Not just from one lily pad to the next - but great big jumping leaps! I am known all over the pond for my jumping. 'Wow! Look at him go! He's the greatest jumper in the pond,' they say.

But I want more. There has to be more.

I'm equipped with poison glands. I will go down fighting if I must. I've heard the horror stories of frogs getting stretched out and pinned down in biology classes, being injected with coloured liquids, even experimented on with electricity! That's no way to go. There's no dignity in that. I hate humans most of all.

Some people think frogs are ugly. This is ridiculous! I'm a fine specimen of a frog. I'd say, even handsome. I see all the females looking at me; wanting to release their eggs in my direction. They are wasting their time. I have no interest in females.

I am intelligent. This is why I am unhappy. It is a curse. It would be easier if I was ordinary. I have dreams, that's my problem. I do not fit in. I'm independent; some call it antisocial. The other frogs are just fat and lazy. I am better than all of them.

When I die, which I eventually will, as we all must - I want to have achieved something; I want to have had a reason to exist.

Someday I hope to travel and see the world. Get far away from here as fast and as my little legs can carry me. I've heard that Paris is a beautiful city and has many fine restaurants and many wonderful cuisines!
It's a big world out there.
There's more to life than this pond.

THE ACTRESS

'Don't call me an actress, you slimy, fat-faced turd; I'm an *actor*; a fully trained and fully professional *actor*, you chauvinistic warty-covered toad!'

Katherine Divine always talked like that. She had a mouth on her like a blocked toilet.

'I understand, I do, I really do,' her agent said, 'but nobody in the business likes you; that's the real problem__'

'When I want your opinion, you four-eyed, spew-flavoured, septic cock - I'll damn well beat it fucking out of you! And keep it up - and I'll smack that cigar you're sucking like a big dick - and ram it up your stretched asshole!'

And that's how it mostly went. A mouth like an overflowing cesspit. Directors, producers, other actors - even the prop men and the catering crew - were all afraid of her. She made grown men cry. And directors and writers pee in their underpants.

She will never get to play James Bond or Rocky Balboa. And she resented that. But she could give us a strong Desdemona or Lady Macbeth; when the mood takes her. If you can get past her demands and her diva-like attitude.

'All I am saying is, a little liposuction, or a bit of plastic surgery - a nip here, a tuck there - would get you more parts; you're not getting any younger__' He was either very brave or very dumb.

Katherine Divine had always looked old. Even in her twenties she played older women (and never had to be made-up to look older). She was no Marilyn Monroe or Kim Basinger. She was never a pinup, or a sex symbol. Not by any stretch of the imagination.

The film critic Leonard Halliwell once described her as: a lesbian, with the body and the face of Quasimodo. 'I said no such thing,' he said, after he finally got discharged from the hospital, 'I merely said she was a thespian; and that her acting embodied the style and the grace of the great Charles Laughton! I would never say anything to offend her. She is a National Treasure!'

Actually, she is more like a cross between Dame Maggie Smith and Mrs. Doubtfire! And, if she's a National Treasure – it's only because she looks like she had once been buried and then dug-up again.

'Do you know who you're talking to - you bloated, cum-filled, ass-licking insignificant grease monkey! I am Katherine Divine! I OWN THE STAGE! I LIGHT UP THE SCREEN! Show me somebody who is better! Nobody - that's who is FUCKING better! The so-called actors today are not worthy to empty my piss pot during intermission! Not one of them has stature, or style, or sophistication! They're all just carbon copy, puffed-up, injected bimbo-fucking porn stars!'

'We can't keep doing this!' said her agent, as he wiped the sweat rolling down his face. 'Are you going to take the part - or are you not going to take the part?'

The part was for her play the Wicked Queen in a pantomime. She would never do that. It was beneath her.

'I'll do it,' she said. 'And your fucking offer better include my upfront fee, a big trailer, a bouquet of fresh flowers every morning, a fruit basket, and a limousine – and, I get to keep all my costumes!'

The panto was a major flop; an unmitigated disaster.
'I think she's got Tourette's syndrome,' said her agent. 'She got away with it in a Pinter play, or when delivering lines like: *Out, Out, Poxy Damn Spot!* - But not in a panto for Christ sake! The poor little kids were traumatised.'

Years later a fan spotted her.
'Look! Look! It's Katherine Divine! I can't believe it! Oh, my God - I can't believe she is working as a waitress!'

It was in a diner on the outskirts of a small town.
'Don't call me a waitress, you stinking piece of cat's vomit; I am a *waiter,* a fully trained and fully experienced *waiter,* you grubby and titless deformed whore!'

The great Katherine Divine looked the part.
But she could not have made many tips.

THE HORRIBLE, UNSPEAKABLE DAY

Rachel Saunders was raped at 9.45pm as she was out walking one Thursday evening in October some years ago. Everything changed after that. In the park where it happened - a pleasant, well-kept park - a sign now says: GATES CLOSE 9PM SHARP.

This is not a blow-by-blow account of what happened to Rachel Saunders that night; it is the telling of what happened to her *after* that night.

She bumped into the rapist one year later in a shopping mall. He looked at her, and smiled, 'Hey, girl, you look familiar, have we met someplace before?' She straightaway went to the toilet and threw up all over her clothes.

The court case was horrible. Most rape victims end up sorry they reported the incident in the first place. It was a horrendous ordeal. The rapist was found not guilty. The usual technicalities, a sharp defending lawyer, and some shoddy police work - all lead to the evidence being inadmissible.

Rachel never took drugs or drank before the rape. Now not a day goes by without her using one or the other to turn her thoughts off, to destroy the pain. She is forever on alert. She is never relaxed. She never lets her guard down.

All happiness, that feeling of safety is gone. Her nervous system is in constant high alert. It is exhausting. There is no reclaiming the happier days before the incident. Everything is tainted by the events of that night. The night Frank Boyle, age 23, decided to have forced sex with a stranger, just because he wanted to.

In court it was said to Rachel, 'Isn't it true that you were not a virgin, and you had had experienced sex many times before the night in question.' She wished she had died that night. This is all wrong, she thought, I have done no wrong. She knew she had lost. No matter what the verdict, or outcome would be: her life had been ruined, and she knew it.

Her father was never able to speak to her about it. He closed down and shut himself off from the whole incident. One night Rachel overheard him in the kitchen talking to her mother: 'How could he have raped her, unless she let him?' The mother slapped the father hard across the face.

Rachel developed eating disorders. In the beginning she hardly ate anything; hoping she would shrink to nothing, and disappear. Then she overate; thinking that if she got extremely large, men would no longer find her sexually attractive.

He took everything from her that night. He took her identity, her reassurance; and her peace of mind. In essence, she has stopped living; she now just exists.

She goes from day to day, to work, and home again. She has no male friends; no male friendships. Men frighten her. It is difficult for her to make eye contact with them; this often makes her appear aloof, distant, or even rude. There is no joy left in her life.

Each night when Rachel turns out the light she is plagued by nightmares and flashbacks. She lies awake questioning her self-worth, her sanity. She constantly blames herself for what happened. She believes she is dirty. That she is damaged goods. 'I should have not froze. I should have fought back. Why did I not scream?'

Finally, she collapses into sleep.

You must put it behind you__
You did nothing wrong__
It was not your fault__
You must move on__
You were one of the lucky ones__
He could have killed you__

All these things were said to her at one time or another.

Time has moved on.
Rachel tries really hard to lead a normal life. Certain sights, sounds, even smells can suddenly bring everything back to her. These are the dark days. 'I am OK. I am OK,' she will repeat to herself. 'It's in the past. It's not happening now. I am not in any danger.'

She hopes someday, she will fall in love, and be able to have sex again. She lives her life the best way she can. No physical tears are left. She is not happy; she is not sad; she gets up every morning - and waits for the days to brighten - to feel good again.

The healing is happening, slowly. But one thing is certain: Rachel will never be forced to do anything - ever again - that she does not want to do.
Even if it means she must die.

THE PLUMBER

Jessica Fawcett is a stunner. There's is no other word to describe her. Men go week just looking at her. They get very excited. They will often call her out to fix a leaky pipe or a dripping tap in the middle of the night. And she'll arrive looking gorgeous. Her makeup applied better than any model.
She is an expert and fully experienced.

Her trick of the trade is to show a bit of a thong or garter belt as she bends down to fix something. She overcharges. But she's worth it. Double the call out fee of her male counterparts. But she looks fantastic. She oozes sex appeal and sophistication. She smells wonderful. She can wear a work-belt like no man alive.

Some people call her a prostitute. The jealous ones. She is a registered, and fully trained plumber. They obviously cannot see past her beauty; and her sexy sensational body.

It is summer. It is hot. He is seventeen. And his parents are away. Stephen has a leak; he needs a plumber. He got Jessica's number from a friend of a friend. She is very busy; but he managed to get a call out for three o' clock tomorrow afternoon.

He has a clogged pip. He blocked it on purpose. What can I say, he's a horny teenager and his hormones are raging. The excitement is too much for him. The photos he saw of Jessica were sensational. He needed a cold shower after looking at them.

Stephen's parents treat him like a kid. 'Do this, do that; don't do this, don't do that.' They nag him all the time. They want him to remain a child. But he can't help it if he is turning into an eager and horny teenager. The time has come. He needs Jessica.

It's two-thirty and Stephen is sweating like a pig. He changed his clothes four times already. He looked at himself in the mirror in his mother's bedroom: 'Is my hair OK? I hope I haven't put too much aftershave on?' The kid is a wreck. 'I can't breathe. What will I say when I open the door! I better not act dumb! This is my big chance! Don't fuck it up! Don't be a douchebag!'

The doorbell rang.

'Hi, I'm Jessica! You must be Steve, I heard you need a service; I'm early, shall we get straight to it!'

Stephen passed out. He fell to the floor.

Jessica had seen this sort of reaction before. That's why she had a bottle of smelling salts with her. When Stephen woke up he was lying on the couch with a wet facecloth on his forehead.

'Where am I? What happened? Did we do anything!' he said, as he tried to sit up; Jessica lay him back down.

'Take it easy; we don't want you to get over excited?' she said, as she gave him a sip of water.

It was all true. No question about it. Jessica Fawcett was the most beautiful woman in the world. The cheek bones. The eyes. The pure perfect figure. Her jeans looked like they were painted on. And her tank top couldn't contain what was bursting out from underneath.

Stephen was in love. All the blood had gone straight to his penis.

'My sink ... I ... I called you about my sink ... I don't know how it happened ... one minute the water went down, then it was all blocked up ... I hope I haven't wasted your time ... do you want a drink or some food - there's some leftover spaghetti in the fridge!'

Jessica smiled, gently patting the boys head with the cold cloth. She held his hand and waited for the colour to come back into his cheeks. Stephen thought he had died and gone to heaven. He hated that his face was full of spots. It made him feel insecure and self-conscious.

They talked for ages. Jessica was a perfect listener.

'I didn't always look like this,' she told him, 'I was once an ugly duckling. When I was about your age I was overweight and I had glasses; I also had a misshapen nose. What you see before you - is artificial. Very little is real.'

Stephen looked at what he saw before him. It was perfect. He wanted to lick and eat every part of it. His excitement was obvious, and hard for him to hide.

'Some years ago,' said Jessica, 'I saw a very beautiful woman walking down the street, and workmen were wolf whistling at her. She did not like it; it annoyed her. I couldn't understand why. I wanted to be whistled at like that. I wanted to be desired as she was. I decided to take control of how I looked.'

Stephen stared at her like an excited puppy. He never thought a real person could be so beautiful, so sexy. He found it difficult to control himself. And then, all of a sudden, it was over.

Jessica said nothing, she just continued talking to him, as he lay back on the couch.

'It takes a lot of work, and a lot of time, to look this good, Steve,' she said. 'It is expensive; it is a work in progress.' Stephen loved her. He loved her honesty.

He may not have fulfilled all of his fantasies that day - but he was happy; he was happy he blocked up the sink; and happy he called Jessica out to fix it. He did not care what it cost. It was his pocket money. He had saved it up. And he could do whatever he wanted to with it.

Stephen never forgot that day.
Today Stephen may not be flush with success - but he has never regretted becoming a plumber. And, no matter how many bad days he is having - or how deep in shit up to his elbows he is - he will always remember how truly sweet Jessica was.

THE COTTAGE INDUSTRY

A few weeks ago I set off on my electric bicycle to visit a premises twenty miles outside of town. My wife had packed me a fine lunch of ham sandwiches, a flask of tea, and a couple slices of lemon drizzle cake. The sun was shining. And I was happy to be out of the office. My name is Douglas Crumb; I work for the Food Safety Authority (the FSA). I'd gotten a call from a woman concerning a business that manufactured dairy products.

I don't drive anymore.

Not since I collided with a mother and pram years ago. The bike is good enough for me now.

The beauty of the unexpected visit is that you can arrive at any time. I could stop at a nice spot on the way and have my lunch. Which I did. I was making good progress. I even got a bit of reading and sunbathing in.

I knew that it was a cottage business, it was home-based, and it employed four staff. They produced milk and cheese products. My job was to make sure the food laws were adhered and all health and safety procedures were in place. It all looked good on paper. It wasn't a mass production or an assembly-line type of business. Meaning: it would be an easy couple of hours for me.

I arrived at three o'clock. I was surprised to find that the business was a convent. Sister Abigail greeted me, and showed me around the garden. It was well kept; they seemed to know what they were doing.

I saw vegetable patches and grape vines. 'Welcome to our humble home,' said the Sister, after she got over the shock of seeing me. 'How may we be of assistance to you and help you on your way?'

I like showing up unannounced. I make sure I have my blue hairnet and white coat on. It makes me look official. It puts people on edge. I'm not the worst Health Inspector around. I work with some right sticklers in the job. They love to come down hard and show their full force of authority. I'm not like that. I'm easy enough to get along with.

Sister Abigail brought me into the kitchen. It all looked fine. Everything was clean. The fridges were at the correct temperature; and there were enough sinks, hand-sanitizers and disposable blue rolls in place. I saw bottles and jars of clotted cream, pro-biotic yogurts, cheeses, and blocks of butter. All very normal.

I noticed the Sister was trying to rush me, edging me nearer the door, all the time.
'Where do you get your milk from that goes into manufacturing this stuff,' I asked. She wouldn't give me a straight answer; she deflected me from the question.
'Oh, we couldn't give our secrets away; let's have some tea and hot crumpets with raspberry jam with some our lovely homemade clotted cream.' I must say they were truly magnificent. I had three of them with a pot of Earl Grey tea.

I didn't go back to the office. I cycled home, and had a rest before dinner. All-in-all it was a very pleasant day. That was Friday.

On the Monday I got another phone call from the concerned woman. She was not happy when I told her everything at the convent was up to standard. 'Go out again!' she said. 'And do a proper job this time! Make sure they show you the whole goddamn place!'
To shut her up I said I would.

A week later I set off to the convent again. I was dreaming about the toasted crumpets and the mouth-watering clotted cream as I cycled. It was a hard cycle. The wind was against me and it was raining. Also, before I left the house my wife had annoyed me, and our dog had had explosive diarrhoea all over the kitchen floor.

This time I had done my homework. I found out that the convent used to be a monastery. It used to be called Beaumont Abbey. Today it is a closed order. The nuns are not allowed to communicate with the outside world. The last time I saw only two nuns. My records show that over forty nuns live there.

I locked my bike to the front gate. (The battery was low as I forgot to charge it the night before. It was a tough cycle home. The bike was like a tank when the battery was dead.) I got out of my wet clothes and put on my blue hairnet and white coat. Sister Abigail saw me from a window and came rushing out.

'What do you want this time?' she said. 'I mean, what a lovely pleasant surprise this is!'
She was not happy to see me.

'I'll be having a much more thorough inspection this time,' I told her. She turned white as a sheet. There was no offer of refreshments this time. After about half an hour of nosing around I asked her if I could use the bathroom. She was all over me like a bad rash; I needed to get away from her and do some investigating.

This is when I heard a moaning sound, combined with a sucking sound, coming from behind one of the doors. The door was locked and had a small window with bars. I looked in and saw a long bench with about thirty nuns sitting on it. They had tubes and pumping equipment attached to them. They were getting milked. The floor was covered with straw; the room looked cold, the walls were whitewashed like an old outhouse or shed.

'Are you lost? The toilet is not on this floor, Mr Crumb,' said Sister Abigail, as she came up behind me, nearly giving me a heart attack. With her hand on my shoulder she walked me to the parlour.

'It's not what it looks like,' she said. 'This is a family run little business we have here.'

This explained why I saw no cows or goats around. I had a few questions about what I saw; was it even legal? I sat with Sister Abigail over a pot of coffee and some baked cheesecake. It was the best and fluffiest cheesecake I've tasted. I could not argue with that.

'You must understand', she explained, 'we are not like other places here, we have a very special and unique way of doing things.'

'But is it legal?' I asked her.

'Absolutely! We are a registered company. All our books are in order.'

'Do the customers know where the milk comes from?' I asked her, as I finished the last slice of cheesecake.

'They know that the products they are buying are the very best on the market and the tastiest around. Don't you know breast milk is full of nutritional goodness? Our nuns pride themselves on the work they do here. It is a vocation. They enjoy it; and they have free range to move around the convent'

I couldn't disagree about the quality. The food they were producing was divine.

'Forgive me if I seem indelicate,' I said, 'but how did the nuns come to produce the milk in the first place?'

'That's the most wonderful part,' she said. 'All the Sisters, over the years, became pregnant for the good of God and mankind! There unselfish, and pure act, gave babies to couples who could not have babies of their own. Our Almighty Father has bestowed these gifts to us.'

I didn't ask where the sperm came from (later I heard local priests were brought in to perform the act). Or how long the nuns were made produce the milk for (some looked very old). Or, if the mass-milking gave the sisters mastitis and sore nipples. (I am not a vet, nor a doctor).

I didn't even ask if they got paid.

This was not my job.

My job was to make sure hygiene standards were adhered to and that the fridges were at the correct temperatures.

I admire the nuns' dedication. They are living a life sanctified by God. They have given a lot and have vowed poverty and obedience. I will keep in contact with Sister Abigail. The convent is a thriving business. I believe they also produce a very good alter wine and gluten-free Communion wafers.

I shall visit again, and keep abreast of the situation.

THE RIP-OFF

The sign says
> DO NOT
> FEED THE
> ANIMALS

Of course I'm not going to feed the animals. I overpaid to come in here in the first place. I'm not going to pay for the animals' food as well. They have more space than we have. More room to roam around. The animals are happy. The visitors not so happy. We have hardly any space. We've narrow roped walkways; they have fabulous open-spaced enclosures. The price of admission is gone up. It's extortion. The staff at the gate should wear balaclavas charging what they do.

I miss the old zoo. Small cages. The animals up-close. Nowhere for them to hide. You were able to feed the monkeys and the elephants. They put a stop to that when one of the elephants chocked on a can of coke. And you used to be able to ride the ponies. That's frowned upon now.

It's like a safari here now. You need binoculars to see the animals. That's when they're not in their huts asleep. They take care of the animals too much. That's what I think. I saw one of the lions getting fed huge lumps of sirloin steak. I'm lucky to get a few sausages at home. That's why they have to charge so much. They don't take short cuts. The animals come first. The customers can go and lump it.

The circus is better. You can sit down and eat candyfloss and popcorn and hotdogs. You see the animals up close. They even do tricks for you. I admit they can often be a bit docile as a lot of them are drugged and have their teeth and claws removed. But the midget clowns are very funny. I'm not mad about the acrobats. They bore me. They cheat and use a net. There's no excitement; no danger. When they fall they just bounce back up again.

Money is hard to come by these days; I want to spend it wisely and get good value. Once you've seen the zoo once, you've seen it enough times. That's what I think. They try and trick you into coming again by getting you interested in a new baby panda or something like that. Not me. And the gift shop is a total rip-off. Soft cuddly toys made in some sweatshop somewhere, sold at ridiculous prices.
They don't fool me. I've been around too long.

The petting corner is also gone. That's a big mistake, a big disappointment. That was my favourite part when I was a kid. I used to love getting to milk a yak, or holding a rabbit up by the ears. I used to love throwing rotten apples and other things at the fat pigs.
It's useless here now. I don't know why I bother. No interaction at all.

I'm saving up to go to Africa. That's where I really want to go. I've wanted to go there since I was a kid. It is expensive. But it will be well worth it.

I've done a heap of research and made a lot of enquiries. I even paid my deposit. This time next year – I'm off to Big Game Hunting in Africa!

Lions, leopards, buffalo, rhinoceroses, elephants! Now, that's entertainment! The BIG FIVE they call them!

I've heard you can eat all you kill, and bring home a trophy, if you can fit it in your suitcase!

Now, I'm excited!

THE UGLIEST WOMAN IN TOWN

Not only had she fallen out of god's ugly tree, and hit every branch on the way down, but her face looked as if had been attacked by a pack of hungry crows. She had red curly hair, freckles, and a lazy eye. And she could peel a pineapple with her overbite. She also never used one word when she could use three. She talked in long and boring sentences.

She worked in the library.
'Have you any books on bird watching?' a customer asked.
'Absolutely definitely indeed we do you will be able to find them located over on the middle shelf in the biology and ecology and environmental section,' she replied.
She irritated people. There was little people could do about it. Jillian Moffatt had verbal vomiting, and a bad case of oral diarrhoea.

As a child she seldom left the house. She would sit under a blanket or behind the curtains and read. She read everything; but she had very little experience of real life. She had poor social skills. In school, she would sit and eat lunch alone, her nose always in a book.

The excessive talking was a symptom of her chronic shyness. If somebody talked to her - or even looked at her - she would go into a hypomanic state of talking. It was involuntary. She had to pinch herself to make the talking stop. She had little burses all over her body.

People never got the chance to have a conversation with her. If Jillian could not hear her own voice, she panicked. Nobody could get past her relentless talking.

She did not speak loudly. But it was never-ending.

The non-stop talking was a control technique she had developed. She hated people to look at her. When she did not have to speak, or look at a person, she felt good; like she was invisible. The spell was broken as soon as a person looked at her, or spoke to her.

When Jillian Moffatt was 8 years old something happened to her. We do not know what it was. We only know that one day her parents had lost her for some hours. (They thought she was safe behind the curtain, reading.) When they eventually found her: she was crying hysterically; she was incoherent and inconsolable.

Today kids in the library make fun of her. Take turns to ask her questions. It's a game they like to play.

'What time does the library close?'

They know what time the library closes. A big sign is on the front door.

'The library closes today at 5 o' clock because today is Friday and will open again at 10 o' clock in the morning but remember tomorrow we shut at 4 o' clock so make sure you gather up all your belongings 15 minutes before hand as we turn off the computers early and we wouldn't want you to be too late to check your books and other items out___'

She pinched herself just below the elbow.

A man once slapped her because she was so boring. (It did stop her talking - but people can't go around slapping other people just because they are boring.) The daily anxiety Jillian suffers is immense. Her symptoms are extreme, and constantly on show. Ordinary interaction is almost impossible for her. She hates her appearance; and the way she talks. A less brave woman would not leave the house in the morning.
　　The god's have not been kind to Jillian Moffatt.

　　But things may improve.
　　Some weeks ago she met a handsome man sitting alone in the braille section of the library. His name is Sam Brown. The man is deaf-blind. (How he stays positive and continues to live every day is a mystery to people.) They hit it off straight away. They have dated now a few times. He has no idea what Jillian looks like. He is unable to hear her continues and tedious ramblings.

　　Yesterday she wore high heel shoes and makeup for the very first time. And a tight pair of jeans. It took a lot of years for Jillian to realise that men notice a woman's backside long before they see her face.

　　She loves her new man. She loves doing things for him. She loves to pamper him and wash him and bring him out for walks.
　　'You're my little angel,' he tells her, 'and you've got a beautiful soul.'

THE AD MAN

I was the best there was. Nobody could touch me. For five decades I was top of the heap, number one; the undisputed king of advertising. People didn't just *see* my ads - they *talked* about my ads! I could sell your granny to the Arabs. Make her beautiful and desirable. Have men lust after her, and drool over her.

That was my job: to make people buy what they didn't want, what they didn't need.

I WAS THE FUCKING MASTER.

I had flare, style. When you saw one of my ads - you *knew* it was my ad! It was never boring or generic. I shocked people. I made them wakeup and open their eyes. I used sex. I used religion. Nothing was sacred. I was the great manipulator. I could misinform and hoodwink better than anyone alive.

Advertisements today are shit.

So sickly sweet, so safe. If they work at all – it's only because people are so fucking dumb.

I used every available media and method to exploit the public. I had no morals. No scruples. My ads were mini masterpieces, works of art. Today they are all banned. This is a compliment. We live in a world of candy-assed, oversensitive bloody snowflakes!

Don't say that__
You can't do that__
That isn't acceptable__

BLAH, BLAH, FUCKING BLAH. I shocked - for the sake of shocking. I made you stare. I turned you on. I got you interested. I sold more products than anyone in the history of advertising. I'm talking useless and unnecessary and worthless products.
    I sold you them all. And you lapped it up.

    I sold you baby formula, I sold you coffins. I sold you mouthwash, I sold you haemorrhoid creams. I squeezed every penny out of you. People love to spend money. That's what I was good at: separating fools from their money.

    This PC world makes me puke. They have barred me from live TV and radio. Because I speak my mind; I tell the truth. I am old and near death now. So I don't give a fuck.
    And if you don't like it – you can go and shove this book you're holding up your hole!

SCARFOLK COUNCIL ADULT SAFETY

CHILDREN CAN & WILL BITE

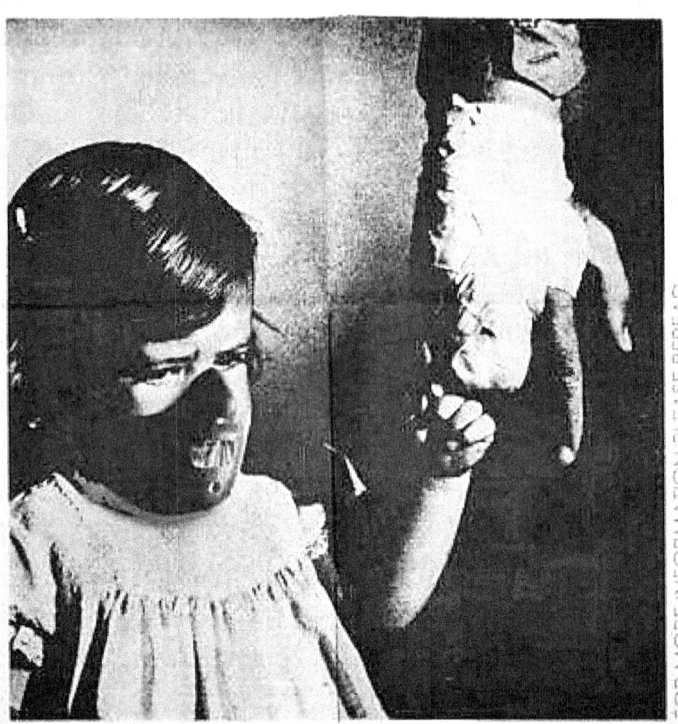

WHEN IN PUBLIC
ALWAYS
REMOVE YOUR CHILD'S TEETH*

*If your child requires its teeth professionally, it must be muzzled at all other times. **Always** carry a medical crowbar. **Always** make sure you are up to date with your tetanus vaccine. **Always** display your minor licence.

FOR MORE INFORMATION PLEASE REREAD

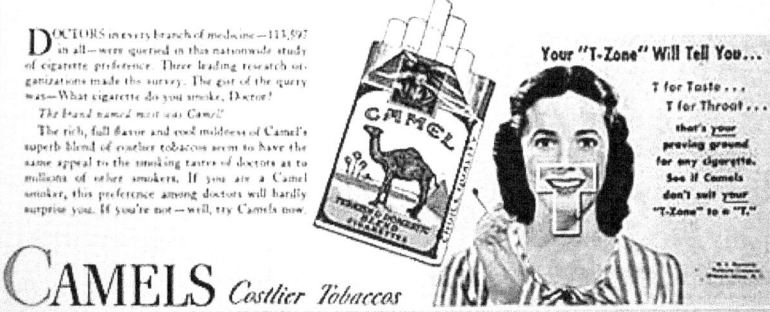

According to a recent Nationwide survey:

MORE DOCTORS SMOKE CAMELS
THAN ANY OTHER CIGARETTE

CAMELS *Costlier Tobaccos*

NICO TIME
CIGARETTES
THE
SMOOTH
TASTE
EXPECTANT
MOTHERS
CRAVE!

Picks up five times more women than a Lamborghini.

BECAUSE BABIES
SHOULD BE SEEN
AND NOT HEARD.
LAUDANUM
CREST
BRAND

"Let's Get Down to Business"

● "STRETCHY-SEAT"† is a Munsingwear' exclusive. It is a special horizontal panel knitted to give *up and down*. No other underwear has "STRETCHY-SEAT." Men find it so comfortable they keep coming back for more. That's good business.

"*Stretchy-Seat*"† *is an exclusive feature of Munsingwear's* SKIT-*Tanks, Shorts, Longies and Shin-highs.*

MUNSINGWEAR'S
"STRETCHY-SEAT"
UNDERWEAR FOR MEN

Advertised in LIFE

MUNSINGWEAR, INC., MINNEAPOLIS · NEW YORK · CHICAGO · LOS ANGELES

MEN'S WEAR

89

"JELL-O' **Pudding Pops**'...
The snack you can say
'Yes' to!"

November 30, 1953

HOOVER

Give her a Hoover and you give her the best

Christmas morning
(and forever after)
she'll be happier
with a Hoover

P. S. to husbands:
She cares about her home, you know, so if you really care about her
... wouldn't it be a good idea to consider a Hoover for Christmas?
Prices start at $60.95. Model 29 (shown here) $95.95. Low down
payment; easy terms. See your Hoover dealer now.

THE HOOVER COMPANY
North Canton, Ohio

"Every morning's a Smirnoff morning."

"They're No.1 for school, gals!"
Jimmy Savile OBE

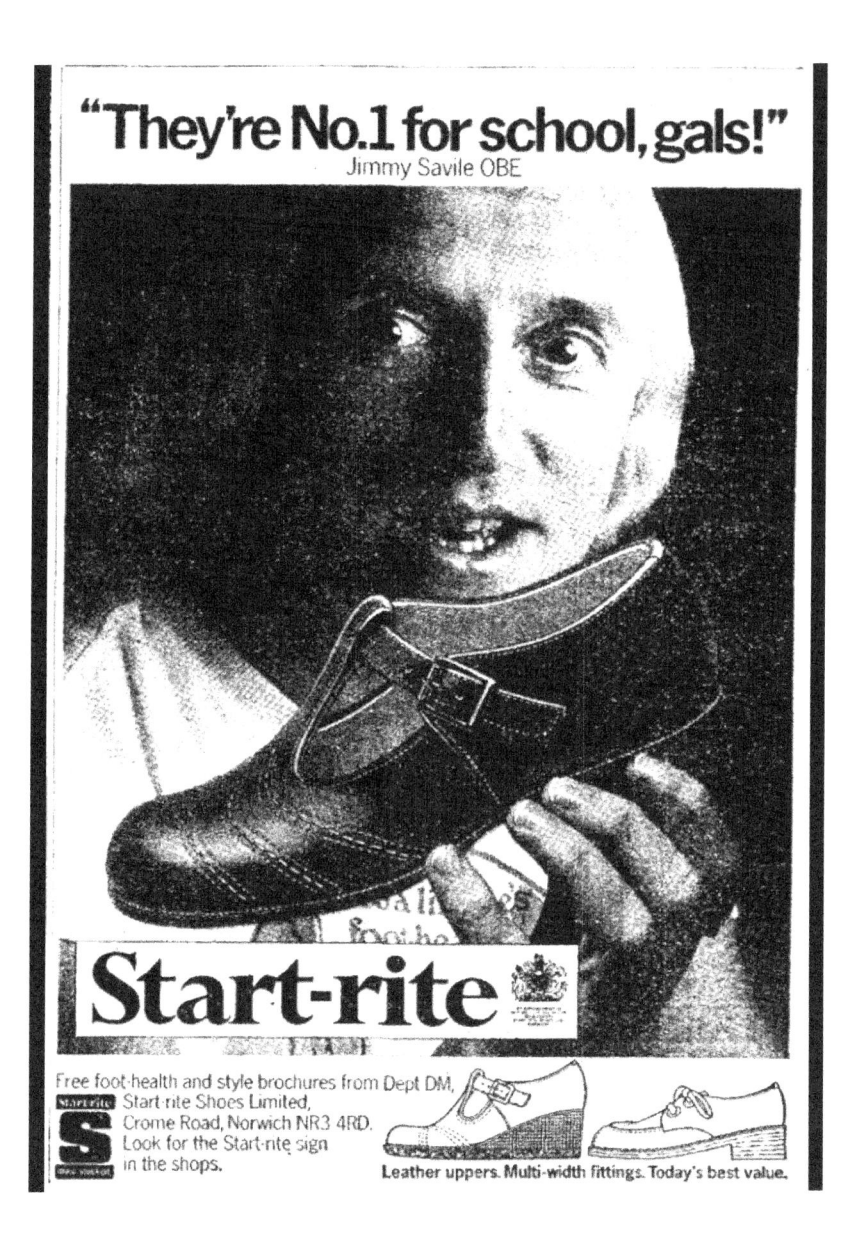

Start-rite

Free foot-health and style brochures from Dept DM, Start-rite Shoes Limited, Crome Road, Norwich NR3 4RD. Look for the Start-rite sign in the shops.

Leather uppers. Multi-width fittings. Today's best value.

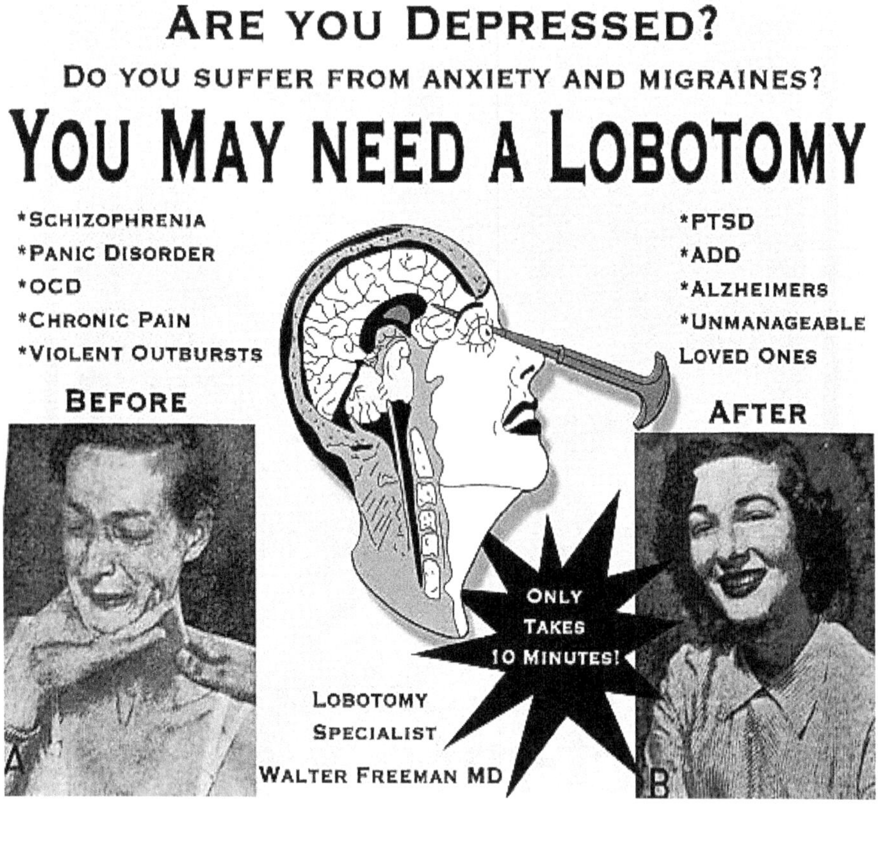

ARE YOU DEPRESSED?
DO YOU SUFFER FROM ANXIETY AND MIGRAINES?
YOU MAY NEED A LOBOTOMY
*SCHIZOPHRENIA
*PANIC DISORDER
*OCD
*CHRONIC PAIN
*VIOLENT OUTBURSTS
*PTSD
*ADD
*ALZHEIMERS
*UNMANAGEABLE LOVED ONES
BEFORE
AFTER
ONLY TAKES 10 MINUTES!
LOBOTOMY SPECIALIST
WALTER FREEMAN MD
A
B

STEVIE WONDER
"If I could play video games, you bet it would be ATARI!"
Stevie isn't superstitious by rule
Only Atari brings the arcade classics home!
Simple, straightforward controllers
You don't need two people to play with an ATARI 2600...Or even two eyes.
ATARI

You can't meet God's gift to women in a singles' bar.

SO THE HARDER A WIFE WORKS, THE CUTER SHE LOOKS!
1. GOSH, HONEY, YOU SEEM TO THRIVE ON COOKING, CLEANING AND DUSTING- AND I'M ALL TUCKERED OUT BY CLOSING TIME. WHAT'S THE ANSWER?
VITAMINS, DARLING! I ALWAYS GET MY VITAMINS
Kellogg's
PEP
Vitamins for pep! PEP for vitamins!*

Constipated
Since Her Marriage

Finds Relief At Last - In Safe
ALL-VEGETABLE METHOD

Where there's Life...there's Bud!
Budweiser
LAGER BEER
AREN'T YOU GLAD? Springtime is a happy time. And the best place to be is close to a Bud. Cold, refreshing Budweiser... the King of Beers.
When you
get her drunk.
Budweiser
CRACKED.COM

SUPER POPS for the ROLF HARRIS
Stylophone & 350S
BOOK 2

by dübreq

Produced for Dubreq Ltd by EMI Music Publishing Ltd.